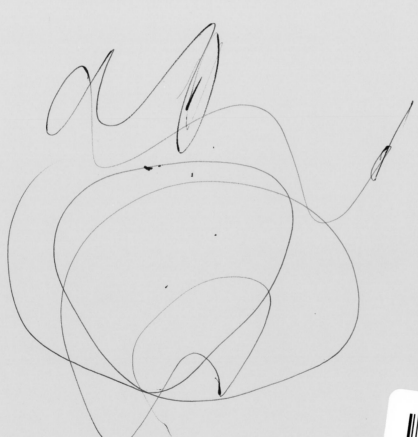

Library of Congress Cataloging-in-Publication Data

Ebie, Mora.
  Going to the zoo in Hawai'i / Mora Ebie ; illustrated
by Jon J. Murakami.
     p. cm.
  Summary: A family walks through Waikiki to visit a
Hawaiian zoo, where they see many exotic animals.
  ISBN-13: 978-1-56647-790-1 (hardcover : alk. paper)
  ISBN-10: 1-56647-790-5 (hardcover : alk. paper)
  1. Honolulu Zoo--Juvenile fiction. [1. Honolulu Zoo--
Fiction. 2. Zoo animals--Fiction. 3. Hawaii--Fiction.] I.
Murakami, Jon J., ill. II. Title.
  PZ7.E1942Goi 2006
  [E]--dc22
                                          2006013986

ISBN-10: 1-56647-790-5
ISBN-13: 978-1-56647-790-1

First Printing, August 2006
Second Printing, July 2007

Mutual Publishing, LLC
1215 Center Street, Suite 210
Honolulu, Hawai'i 96816
Ph: (808) 732-1709
Fax: (808) 734-4094
email: info@mutualpublishing.com
www.mutualpublishing.com

Printed in Korea

**With warm aloha,
I thank John, Ellen,
and Meredith Ebie.**
—Mora Ebie

Today we are going
to the zoo.
To get there, we walk
through Waikīkī.

Lifeguards in red board shorts watch the surfers and swimmers play in the blue waves.

The pink hotel on the beach matches the pink lei on Duke Kahanamoku's statue.

I wave to policemen on bicycles, and they wave back.

We run under a big banyan tree in front of the zoo.

Inside the zoo, the first animal we see is a flamingo. Flamingoes are from the Caribbean Islands. The shrimp they eat turn their feathers pink.

I like the elephant. The elephant is from India. Elephants have the biggest brains in the animal kingdom.

Look at the monkeys! They are from Africa. Monkeys can climb small trees when scared, and can run fast on the ground to escape from danger.

The alligator is from Florida.
Alligators like to eat bugs, frogs,
snakes, fish, and even deer
or cows.

The sun bear is from Southeast Asia. They are playful as young cubs.

The hippo is from Africa. An adult hippo eats more than 150 pounds of grass a day.

Next, we visit the antelopes and gazelles. Antelopes and gazelles are from Africa. They have horns permanently attached to their heads.

The zebra is from Africa.
Adult zebras are black and
white, but baby zebras are
brown.

Wow! A giraffe! The giraffe is from Africa. The giraffe's tongue is black and she can grow up to eighteen feet tall.

The cheetah is from Africa.
A cheetah can run up to 70 miles
per hour in less than a minute.

The lion is from Africa. The lion's mane makes him appear larger than he really is and protects his neck when he fights with other lions.

The tiger is from the island of Sumatra. The tiger likes to swim and his stripes help hide him in the tall grass.

It's Rusti and Violet! Orangutans live in the tropical rainforests on the islands of Borneo and Sumatra. They build nests in trees when they want to sleep.

We can't forget to visit the Nēnē, Hawaiʻi's state bird.

It is getting late. On our way to the petting zoo, we see a peacock. I love his blue and green feathers.

Hello Lani Moo!
Lani Moo is a big brown
and white cow. She weighs
over 1,200 pounds.

It is time to leave the zoo.
I will miss the animals, but we
will visit again.